Magic Fairy Stories

Magic Fairy Stories

Edited by Susan Taylor

Illustrated by Severino Baraldi

WARD LOCK LIMITED · LONDON

Contents

First Published in Great Britain 1972 by Ward Lock Limited,
166 Baker Street, London W1M 2BB

Printed by Leefung-Asco Printers Ltd., Hong Kong.

ISBN 0 7063 1696 7

The
Glass
Box

Once upon a time there were three poor girls who lived alone in a little cottage. The two older sisters were jealous and bad-tempered, and hated housework above everything.

The youngest was very beautiful and suffered a good deal at the hands of her sisters. As they were talking one day beside the open window, she said to them, 'Yesterday evening, as I was going to bed, a most beautiful bird flew into my room. It could speak just like a man and it told me that one day I should be Queen and have three beautiful children, two boys and a girl. And it told me that the girl would have a golden star on her forehead.'

The two sisters laughed. 'You've dreamt it all,' they said, and they made fun of her.

However, the young King was standing under the window and heard the whole conversation. He knocked on the cottage door, walked in, and stood before he youngest girl. He apologised for his hasty entrance and begged the youngest sister to become his wife. She blushed and said she was too poor and lowly; but she said it so charmingly that he liked her even more and repeated his request. She made the excuse that she could not leave her sisters there alone and so he said, 'Bring them also,' and so all three followed him.

Soon the wedding day came. The young King's people were delighted with

their beautiful new Queen, and did not mind a bit that she came from a lowly background. It made her seem closer to them, and she certainly did not put on airs and graces as her sisters did.

The wedding was a wonderful affair. The young Queen wore a white dress of pure silk, with orange blossoms tied in her golden hair. She and the King rode to church in a lovely horse-drawn carriage, and the streets were lined with cheering crowds, for the King had proclaimed a public holiday and all were out to see the new Queen pass. The two sisters rode behind; their faces were sour and they frowned at the crowds and would not wave to them, for each was full of jealousy and wished above everything that she was to be Queen instead of the young sister, and not just a lady-in-waiting at the court.

After the wedding there was a great feast in the gardens of the castle, and when all had eaten their fill there was dancing under the stars to the music of a hundred violins.

The youngest sister made a good Queen, for she had a natural grace and dignity, and she spent many hours doing good works among the poor. She even sold some of her jewellery so that she could buy them meat when the harvest was bad. Her sisters chided her for this, saying she was too ignorant to know the value of her jewels, but she only laughed and said, 'My husband the King did not marry me for baubles. I was clad only in a rough shift when he asked me to be his wife.'

Then her sisters would toss their heads and hurry away to lock their jewels in the safest oak chests they could find for they feared the Queen might ask them to sell their rings and bracelets too if there were another famine.

A year passed and the Queen was going to have a child. There was much rejoicing throughout the land, and all hoped that the Queen would have a boy who would grow up brave and strong and be a good heir to their present King.

The King, however, had to go to war. He called the two sisters and ordered them to look after the Queen and to care for the baby when it came. Then he left.

As the Queen's time drew near, the sisters would allow no one to enter her room, and made her stay there all alone, eating only bread and milk, for this, they said, would assure her of a healthy baby boy.

They gave her a sleeping draught just before the baby came and afterwards they took the infant away. They stole out of the castle that night and carried it to a poor man and his wife who had no children of their own, gave them money so they could bring the boy up, and warned them never to enquire about the background of this child.

When the Queen awoke from her sleep she found a small dog in the cradle in-stead of the long-awaited baby. She cried out in alarm and wept bitterly, and the sisters moaned and said to her, 'God has punished you for your pride and given you a dog instead of a baby.'

The Queen was most distraught, and wondered what she could tell her husband when he returned. At last the war was over and when the King came back and

discovered that the Queen had presented him with a dog instead of an heir to the throne he was very sad, but because he loved his wife he closed his lips tightly and said nothing; but there was a sad, puzzled expression in his eyes whenever he looked at his wife. However, he brought up the little dog and always kept it close by him.

When the Queen was awaiting a second child it was once again wartime and the King went off to fight. And once more history repeated itself. When he returned he again found a dog in the cradle. But he said nothing and brought the dog up as a child.

His people did not dare to say anything out loud, but secretly among themselves they whispered that the Queen was a witch and it would be a good thing to have her burnt, for they were afraid the evil might spread to themselves.

It was a difficult time of war just then, and at the birth of the third child the King was away again. This time, when he returned, he found a cat in the cradle.

Then his patience snapped, and, determined to make an end of this witchcraft, as he thought it to be, he sent the Queen away from court and ordered her never to return. He was very unhappy to have to do this, but it was the advice of his chief ministers and he saw the wisdom of it. The Queen kissed her sisters and thanked them humbly for all their help during her childbirths. Then she left, crying bitterly, and took the cat with her.

However, before she left, she went to a wise man and asked for his advice. 'I cannot help you,' he said, 'but at the edge of this country, in the Sea of Stone, in a gap between two rocks, lives a talking bird who knows everything. It will be able to tell you what to do.'

He gave her a round glass box in which there was a golden arrow, and continued, 'Follow wherever the arrow points and you will find the Sea of Stone and the talking bird. But take care. You must not turn round when you get to the Sea of Stone, otherwise you will immediately turn into stone yourself.'

The Queen promised to take great care, took her cat, and started on her journey, always following the golden arrow. The road was long, and it took the Queen many days to reach the Sea of Stone. She was footsore and hungry, and her clothes were torn and dirty. But the little cat walked by her side and listened as she told it of her sorrow, and rubbed its soft head against her ankles in sympathy.

On the way the Queen stopped and knocked on a cottage door to ask for some milk for the cat and a little water for herself. An old, bent woman answered, and when she saw the Queen and the little cat she drew them inside and brought them many wonderful things to eat and drink.

Then the old woman said to the Queen, 'I know who you are, your Majesty, and I have heard of the misfortune which befalls you. If you wish I can conjure up a whole plague of locusts which will destroy all the land of that wicked man, your husband. But first you must give me your magic box.'

But the Queen only shook her head, saying, 'You have been most kind to me, but that I shall not do. I could neither part with the box nor bring ill upon my unhappy husband. He did only what he thought was right, and it was I who brought such troubles on his head.'

Then the old woman screamed and cursed, and the Queen ran out of the cottage in a fright, and the cat came scurrying after her, its hair on end and its tail like a fat bush.

Next the Queen came upon a group of gypsies camping in a wood. They were singing and dancing while the women stirred a huge pot from which came all sorts of wonderful smells. They invited the Queen to join them, and this she gladly did. She and the little cat sat by the fire and ate the most delicious stew they had ever tasted.

Then the oldest and most cunning of the gypsies grasped the Queen's hand and said, 'Dear lady, we know your mission and your misfortune. One so pretty should not suffer. Let us therefore help you. We will send wild horsemen into your husband's land, and they will ride through the crops and steal the hens and burn down all the houses. That would be a fitting punishment indeed. But first you must give me your magic box.'

But the Queen only shook her head sadly. 'That I could never do,' she said. 'I love the King my husband with all my heart, and his people, too, are very dear to me. Why should I bring suffering to them when it was I who caused such trouble in the first place?'

Then the gypsies began to shout and rage and they threw sticks at the Queen and her cat and chased them away out of the wood.

Three more times this happened on the way, and at last the Queen decided to avoid all human company, for there was no one she could trust.

When she reached the Sea of Stone, she

...ddenly heard behind her many voices which whispered and laughed and screamed. The cat took fright, pulled away, and ran back, and as the Queen turned round to look for it they were both turned to stone.

Now you will remember that the Queen's three children had been taken to a poor couple to be cared for. These three were now almost grown up. The two boys were very handsome and strong, and the girl was beautiful and delicate. She had a golden star on her forehead.

Then suddenly the foster-mother died, followed shortly afterwards by her husband. As he felt his end was near he called all three children together and said to them, 'You think, my dears, that I am your father, but this is not so. You were brought to me when you were very small. Who you are I have never discovered. I do not even know whether you are related. From your looks I would assume that you are. Perhaps you can discover the truth.'

And he told them about the wise man to whom they should go for advice. Then he closed his eyes and died and they mourned for him as if he had been their own father.

Soon after his death the children decided to visit the wise man as he had told them. The wise man gave them the same advice as he had given the Queen and warned them not to turn round on the way and to go singly as it would be safer. He gave each of them a glass box with a golden arrow and wished them luck in their quest.

The eldest went first. Like his mother, he met many people on the way who wanted to trick him out of his magic box, but he refused to part with it. He soon reached the Sea of Stone, but while he was searching for the talking bird he heard behind him the sound of many

voices. These voices laughed and called and seemed to beckon him and, as he took no notice, one voice suddenly shouted, 'You are going the wrong way, young man. Look, this is the right road.'

Then he forgot, turned round, and immediately he was turned to stone.

His brother and sister waited in vain, and at last the sister said, 'Something must have happened to our brother. I will go and look for him.'

But the younger brother did not agree and set off himself, taking no notice of those who tried to stop him and get the magic box.

But he fared no better than his brother, and his sister soon realised that he too had not been successful. So she set off, and soon found the Sea of Stone and entered it bravely.

She ignored the voices, however much they tried to entice her, and she could already see the gap in the rock when she heard a voice behind her which sounded like that of her elder brother; and it called, 'Here, sister dear, I am here; come this way!'

She stood still and listened. Again she heard a voice behind her and it sounded like the voice of her second brother 'Sister, I am here!'

But she was not deceived. She had already seen the beautiful bird. She approached it and stretched out her hand towards it. Then there was a sudden hush, and she heard its voice which said, 'Take your mug and draw water from this spring. Then drop one drop on to each stone which you see here around you.'

She did as the bird commanded her. Then one stone after another came to life; men stood up and then women, knights and soldiers with horses and weapons; all of whom had been turned to stone on the way to the talking bird. Women and children from all walks of life and from all ages of time stretched their limbs and took their first stumbling steps since they were turned to stone long, long ago.

And now a stone began to move which turned out to be her elder brother, and then another one and this was her

younger brother, and they embraced and laughed and cried with sheer happiness.

Not far away stood a woman with sad eyes. She had a little cat with her and both had just come to life again. The children did not recognise the Queen, their mother, of course, for they were babies when they were taken from the castle.

She, however, saw the golden star on the girl's forehead, and then she remembered what the talking bird had told her on that night so long ago; and now it began to speak again and said, 'These three are your rightful children.'

The Queen was filled with joy, and wept for her good fortune. Then she dried her tears and hurried over to the children and embraced them. At first they could not grasp what this unknown lady wanted

from them, but she began to ask them questions and to tell her story, and then they told her how they had lived till now.

They talked for a long time, the Queen asking eager questions and the children telling her how happy they had been, and how well their foster-parents had cared for them.

When she heard that both were now dead, the Queen looked sorrowful again. 'I am sorry for that,' she said. 'It would have pleased me to see these people and to thank them for all that they have done.'

And she grew even more sorrowful as she realised it was her own two sisters who had stolen her babies away and put the dogs and the cat in their places. 'I must have hurt them badly at some time,' she said, 'for them to take such terrible revenge.'

Then they all hugged and kissed one another again and began to make plans for their return home.

The knights and soldiers who had come to life again were standing around and listening. Some of them had heard about the Queen's sad life, and soon they all agreed that they should accompany the Queen back to the King and tell him the whole story so that he would reinstate her as Queen.

They formed themselves into two long lines, with the Queen and her children and the cat in the front, and with much

shouting and cheering the procession set off.

The King had not forgotten his wife and was often very sorry that he had sent her away. The two dogs which he took to be his children had both died.

At last the many wars were finally finished and his chancellor and ministers persuaded him to remarry so that the country would have a crown prince, and at length he was persuaded to become engaged to the eldest sister.

As the bells were ringing and he wa driving with his bride to the church, troop of knights and soldiers came alon the road. At their head walked the Quee with her three children, and even the ca was with them. The King halted th carriage and got out, for he had recog nised his wife, and she came nearer smiling, and pointed to her beautifu grown-up children.

'These are the animals I bore you,' he said. The King did not understand and he looked questioningly from one to the other, from his wife to his bride.

The talking bird appeared and sang a song about the king who went to war three times and each time a child was exchanged by his wife's sisters. The King questioned the two sisters and asked them if the bird was speaking the truth. They could not deny it because there stood the scorned Queen as a witness.

Then he ordered that both the sisters be put in chains and called for judges who pronounced the sentence. They should be led to the Sea of Stone and made to turn round and thus be turned to stone themselves. The Queen, however, fell on her knees before him and said, 'My dear husband, will you, after all this time, grant me my first wish?'

'Speak,' said the King. 'I will grant

you anything, so long as you forgive me.'

So the Queen said, 'These two are my sisters, and for the sake of my dear parents, please forgive them.'

Then the King said, 'Now I know for certain that it is you. You were always kind and forgiving.' And he embraced her.

Then there was a great feast and both sons were knighted and the daughter married the King of a neighbouring country, and everywhere was peace and happiness.

The talking bird sang at the feast for all it was worth, and then, as dawn crept through the castle windows, it flew far away into the blue, well satisfied with its work, and was never seen again.

The Magic Thread

Once upon a time there was a widow who had a son called Peter. They lived together at the edge of the village in a wooden house which she had been left by her husband. He had died soon after Peter was born, so she had to work hard to look after her son and keep him in all the clothes and toys a small boy needs and wants. Fortunately, Peter was a strong, practical boy, and he spent much of his spare time helping her to clean and shop, chop wood and tend the garden. He was also an intelligent boy, only he did not like going to school, in spite of the fact that he learned quickly and easily. His thoughts were always wandering.

Sometimes he would sit at his desk and his mind would drift to the days when he would be on holiday, playing round the cottage with his little dog, Sandy. On other days he would think of Christmas, with its cold and snow, the warm log fire, good food and exciting presents. And on other days, when he was in a world of his own, he would not have been able to tell you what he had been thinking of had you asked him, for he would think of nothing in particular for hours.

One day, he was sitting in his history class. He was not listening at all, for if anything bored him it was the past. His thoughts were always of the future, and of his place in it.

Suddenly his teacher interrupted his thoughts. He had been dreaming of the time when he would be grown-up and earning his own living. He would be rich and successful and able to buy his mother a bigger cottage, and pay someone from the village to help her with the work.

'Peter, what are you thinking about now?' the teacher asked him.

'I was thinking what I would do when I was grown-up,' answered Peter.

'Can't you wait?' said the teacher. 'Surely you are happy enough now. When one is grown-up everything is by no means perfect.'

But Peter found it difficult to wait. When winter came and he was sliding over the frozen lake, he was thinking 'If only it were summer', and when summer came, he was longing for the autumn so that he could fly his kite on the village green. In autumn his thoughts were only of the beauty of spring, when the flowers and trees were bursting into life. But come the spring, and Peter's mind was already on winter, with its crisp mornings and mysterious, frost-laden nights. When he sat in school in the morning, he wished it were already evening, and on Sunday evening in bed he sighed, 'If only the holidays started tomorrow.'

Peter had many friends at school, for despite his dreaminess and impatience he was full of fun and ideas for new games. Sometimes he would play with all the boys of the village, chasing a ball across the streets and kicking a stone from gate-post to gate-post. Sometimes he would go hunting with his friends, and if they were lucky they would return with a nice juicy rabbit for their supper.

But Peter enjoyed playing with his friend Lisa most. She was a year younger than he and her parents lived nearby him. She was a very good runner, just like a boy, and did not get offended even if he was sometimes very impatient with her. Often when she came to fetch him he thought:

'If only I were grown-up, then I would marry Lisa.'

Sometimes he did not want to see

anybody. Then he would wander alone in the woods thinking deep thoughts.

At last it was summer time, and Peter had a long holiday ahead of him. For several weeks now he would not have to wish that the days would pass quickly, though sometimes, when it was too hot, he would think of playing with his kite in the strong wild winds of autumn.

First thing in the morning he helped his mother wash the breakfast dishes, and then he scrubbed the floor. Just for a moment he did begin to wish the morning over, for although he did not mind helping in the house he could see through the kitchen window his friends setting off to the river with their fishing rods, and he longed to go with them.

Then, in the afternoon, he went to the woods to explore. He had been wandering around for a long while and now he lay

day-dreaming in the hot sun in a little clearing. Soon he stopped thinking and fell asleep. He slept deeply for a long time, and it was almost dark when he was awakened by the sound of someone calling his name.

Peter was startled. He knew all the people of the village, and this woman was a complete stranger. He was wide awake now, and not a little afraid, for the woman was oddly dressed and her eyes looked in different directions. But she smiled quite pleasantly at the boy and spoke in a friendly fashion.

'Oh, Peter,' she said, 'it is never the right time for you, is it? I have often heard you wishing your precious days away. But never mind, I have here something to help you if you want it. Look!'

She had a little silver box in her hand. It was as round as a ball and from a small hole came the end of a very fine gold thread.

'Do you see this thread?' she asked. 'This is the thread of your life. If you want the time to pass quickly, pull at the thread. If, however, you want it to take as long as it does for other people, then leave it alone. But let me give you a word of advice. Don't pull it too often or too hard; just one tiny little pull and an hour or two is past. Remember, you can never push it back in when you have pulled it out. It just disappears like smoke. Never tell a single person in the whole world that you have this, for on that day you

will die. Now tell me, Peter, do you want it?'

Peter looked at the woman wonderingly. Never had he dreamed of such a gift. Why, boredom, fear, and pain would be banished in an instant with the help of the little ball. He nodded at the old woman.

'Oh yes, please,' he said. 'Oh I do; please, let me have it!'

Peter stretched his hand out greedily for the silver ball. It was quite light and small, but firm, as if made in one piece. There was only the one small hole from which hung the golden thread.

When he looked up again the old woman had disappeared. Peter held the ball in his hand and looked at the thread. It seemed to him as if the thread was coming very, very slowly out of the hole, but it did not become any longer. He would have liked to have pulled it a little bit, but he was rather frightened.

When he was in his bed that night he wondered whether he should pull out enough of the thread to make him grown-up, but he remembered what the old woman had said, and left it alone.

But the next day, at school, when he was not paying attention, his teacher scolded him, and now Peter could not resist any longer. Very, very carefully he pulled the thread out a little bit, and immediately the teacher said it was time to go home.

He soon did this quite often—in fact, every day—and life was wonderful. He had lots of free days, for as soon as school came in sight, he pulled the thread a little. He did not do it during the holidays, but wandered around in the woods and tried to decide when he could pull it again, or he played with Lisa. This went on for some time.

Unfortunately, missing so much school, Peter did not learn a great deal, but this

lid not worry him one bit. Most of all in life he loved to be out in the open air and he was now able to spend nearly every fine day out playing. Sometimes he was tempted to tell Lisa of his magic ball, but always he remembered, just in time, the old woman's warning, and so he kept the secret.

One day he thought: 'I am really rather silly. These ceaseless holidays are a little boring. If I were grown-up and had left school, I could quickly learn my trade and marry Lisa, and then I would not need to pull at the thread very much any more.'

He thought about this scheme for several days before he finally determined to leave his childhood days for ever.

During the night he pulled out quite a long piece of thread and the next morning he was already apprenticed to a carpenter, for this was what he wanted to be as his father had been before him.

Peter really enjoyed life now. He was free from the tedious days of the classroom, and able to spend all the daylight hours out in the open air. He climbed around on scaffolding and roofs and carried the heavy planks of wood, and happily hammered nails into the beautiful sweet-smelling timber. Only very seldom, if pay day was too long in coming round, did he pull the thread a little bit, and then it was the end of the week.

But as soon as he had learnt everything he became impatient. Lisa was not here

any more. She had gone to an aunt in the city to learn to cook and care for a house and husband, so he often had to travel into the city to see her. These journeys were tiresome to Peter. He had to walk many miles to the house where Lisa was staying, and often he did not return home until midnight. After a long day's work such visits soon tried his patience.

So, when he was sure he could earn enough money to support the two of them, he asked Lisa to become his wife.

'Of course,' she said, 'but I must remain here another year and learn so that you will have a good wife.'

'Oh well,' said Peter and smiled to himself, 'this year will pass quickly,' and he went back to his building site.

The more he thought of marriage to Lisa, the more he felt that a year was far too long to wait. Once he was married to his childhood friend he felt sure he would have no need of the magic ball. At last his patience got the better of him.

During the night he could not sleep and finally, unable to wait a moment longer, he pulled the thread. And in the morning, with the passing of the night, the year had also passed and Lisa stood there laughing up at him, and there were only six weeks to wait before the wedding.

Now Peter was happy; but not for long. The postman came and brought a blue letter which told Peter he had to go and be a soldier for two years. Peter showed Lisa the letter and she said that really the two years would pass quite quickly provided there were no wars, and Peter said laughingly: 'I think so, too.'

When he was in the barracks he didn't immediately pull the thread, for he was quite content among the young men; he thought about what the old woman had told him and waited a while, even when his service became more exacting.

Then he began to pull the thread again so that his leave should come round, and when he returned to the barracks he did not enjoy the army any more. Every morning he pulled the thread a little bit more and finally even on Sundays when he was having fun with his mates. So his army service passed quickly like a dream and even Lisa was surprised how soon it finished.

When he got home, Peter made a firm decision not to pull the thread again. For now, said his mother, was the best time of his life and this should not pass too quickly; but still, from time to time before the wedding, if he felt he was working too hard on the scaffolding, he pulled it a tiny little bit. But his life was nearly the same as other people's and he often thought proudly: 'If only they knew what I can do!'

On the wedding day everybody was very happy and Peter guarded against any form of impatience, although he could hardly wait to bring his Lisa to the beautiful little house he himself had built for her. At the wedding feast he looked up and noticed that his mother, who was sitting at the table with a neighbour and chatting happily, had a lot of grey hairs, and his conscience pricked him because he had pulled the thread so often. He now had every intention of pulling the thread as seldom as possible.

Everything went smoothly for a few months, till Lisa told him that they were

going to have a child. Peter could hardl
wait for this event, so the thread wa
pulled again. At last the child arrived
and Peter was full of joy and excitemen
But he could not bear it when the bab
cried or was ill, so he pulled the threa
quite often now. He even pulled it s
that the time when the child could tal
and run about would come more quickly

For a time business was bad. He coul
not stand this. After all, it was for thi
sort of situation that he had his magi
thread. People generally become dis
satisfied when there is little work an
money about.

Then for a time there were wicke
people who ruled the land, and the
wanted to change everything throug
force; anyone who said anything agains
them was either killed or put into priso
Peter was used to saying what he though
and so one day they came to fetch hin
also and the fact that Lisa cried, an
begged them to leave him with her an
the child, helped not a bit. So it was ver
lucky Peter had his little silver ball t
hand. Hardly had they taken him awa
than he pulled and pulled, so that hi
enemies were swept away as if in a sand
storm. Then there was a war, but this
too, passed as if it were a short shar
thunderclap, and Peter found he wa
once again with his family; but it ha
cost him many years of his life.

Now all was well and Peter was ver
careful for a long time not to pull th

thread. One morning he noticed that the thread was no longer golden but silver and he suddenly realised that it would not last for ever.

Peter and Lisa lived happily together and he began to think he would have no further use for the ball. But Lisa gave him more children. They were lively and mischievous, and always in need of new clothes and more food. Even Lisa, though she loved her children, sometimes complained that they were too much for her and wished they were off her hands.

One night, when he again lay awake for a long time, he thought that it would indeed be much nicer if the children were all grown up and well established, and so once again he gave a terrific pull of the thread till they had all happily left home; and now Peter too had silver hairs on his head.

All this had not taught him patience; if he had toothache or if his rheumatism was particularly painful when he was working, he was not long suffering, but helped himself in the only way he knew. Lisa had many illnesses; this too he could not accept and once more he had to resort to his magic thread.

So life passed more and more quickly. He could drive away his difficulties, but there were always new ones. However much he pulled at his magic thread life was never as it had been before and never quite perfect. At length his work became too much for him. His bones ached as he

clambered around on the scaffolding, and he was slower and slower in fulfilling his orders.

Still Peter struggled on. He was a grandfather now, and it amused him to hear his little grandson, who was only three, say: 'Oh dear, I can't wait to go to school with my brothers and cousins,' or: 'I can't wait till I am big and can build houses like you, Grandfather.'

His mother died, and Peter felt he could not bear the sadness, but this was one grief he determined to brave alone, without the help of the magic thread, for he had loved her dearly. She had been very old when she died, and scarcely strong enough to care for herself and her little cottage, but she had refused to leave home and come to live with her son and daughter-in-law.

Often Peter would sit in the doorway of his cottage on summer evenings, smoking his pipe and gazing out over the fields, dreaming.

Now, his thoughts were not always of the future, for when he thought of that he realised the end was not far off, and he was afraid. Instead, like all old people, he took refuge in the past.

But poor Peter! He had not many memories to feed his mind now. His life had passed all too quickly and pleasure had come so thick and fast. No sooner had one gone than another came, and he was hard put to it to remember them all. And he could not look back, as other men do, and say to himself: 'Now that was a moment to be proud of—that was a difficult time I struggled with and overcame,' or 'Those were hard days, but my misfortunes taught me many things.'

One morning Peter noticed the thread was not silver but grey.

He looked across at his wife and saw that she was bent and tired. He glanced in the mirror and saw that his hair had grown thin on top and that his face had many wrinkles, so he said to himself: 'Now we shall have to slow down.'

This pleased Lisa, who felt he ought to retire. Business had been bad for several years. Clients complained because their roofs were not repaired before the winter came, and gates were left hanging off their hinges so that the sheep and cattle escaped. Next day Peter went into the little hut which was his office, and told his son that he would have to leave the work to him in future.

'You have learnt well,' he said, 'and

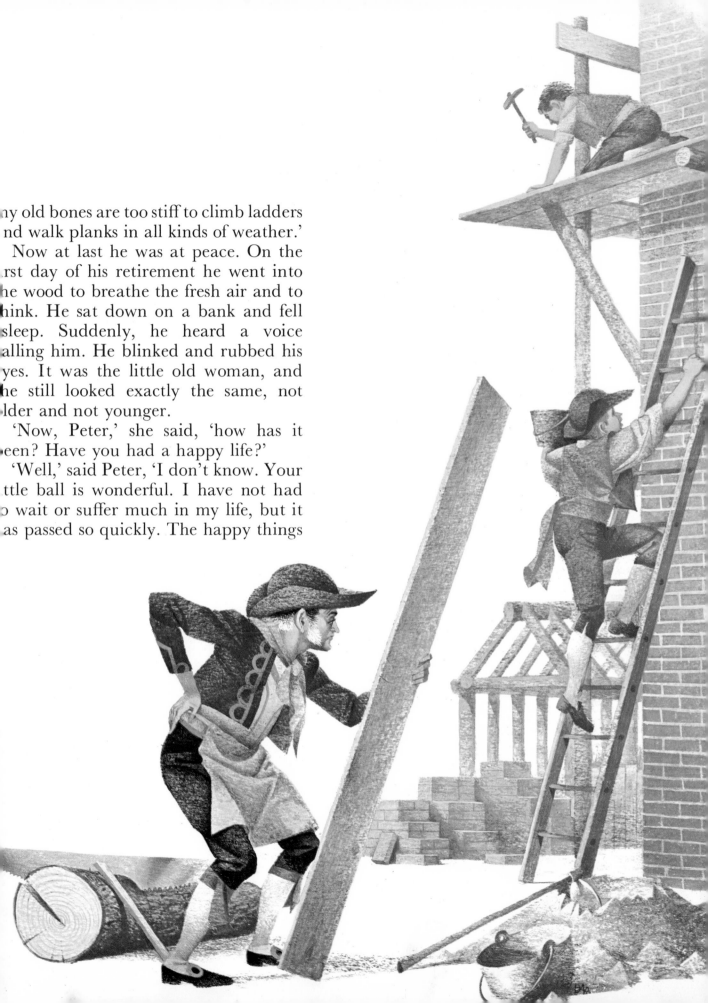

ny old bones are too stiff to climb ladders
nd walk planks in all kinds of weather.'

Now at last he was at peace. On the
rst day of his retirement he went into
he wood to breathe the fresh air and to
hink. He sat down on a bank and fell
sleep. Suddenly, he heard a voice
alling him. He blinked and rubbed his
yes. It was the little old woman, and
he still looked exactly the same, not
lder and not younger.

'Now, Peter,' she said, 'how has it
een? Have you had a happy life?'

'Well,' said Peter, 'I don't know. Your
ttle ball is wonderful. I have not had
o wait or suffer much in my life, but it
as passed so quickly. The happy things

came swiftly one after the other; but I was always impatient and wanted it still better, and now I am old and feeble. I do not dare to pull any more so that things would improve. I suppose I have nothing to complain of, but even now my life is far from perfect. Your gift has not brought me happiness.'

'My, my,' said the little woman. 'You are not very grateful; but tell me, how should it have been different?'

'You should have given me another little ball,' said Peter. 'One whose thread could have been pushed back, then I could have improved on my mistakes, and life would not have passed so quickly.'

'Heh, heh,' said the little woman, 'unfortunately this cannot be done. God does not permit it; but I can grant you one wish, you spoilt creature. Think har[d] what you would like most of all.'

So Peter gathered his thoughts togethe[r] and said: 'I should like to relive my lif[e] but without your magic ball, because [I] am sure I would again pull the threa[d] too often. I want to live like other peopl[e.] If all goes well, let it be so, and if thing[s] hurt, let them hurt.'

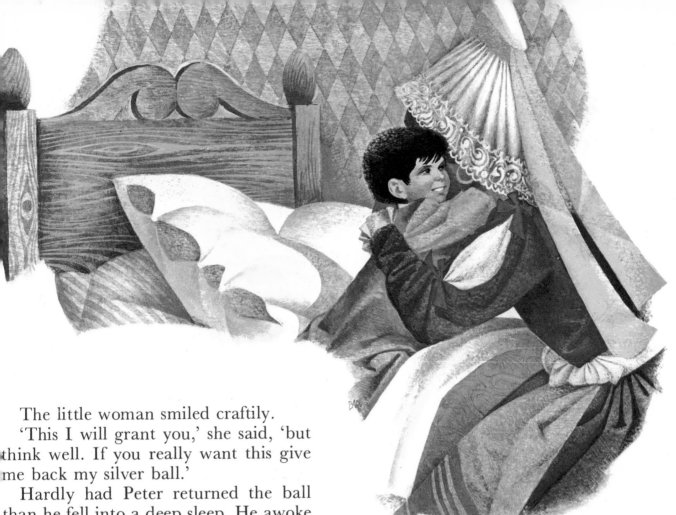

The little woman smiled craftily.
'This I will grant you,' she said, 'but think well. If you really want this give me back my silver ball.'

Hardly had Peter returned the ball than he fell into a deep sleep. He awoke in his bed; his mother was sitting beside him and she was not old and grey, but young and fresh. She looked at him lovingly and said: 'Have you woken up at last, Peter?'

'Where am I?' he asked.

'In your bed, of course, you silly boy. You have had a bad fever,' replied his mother. 'You were too long in the woods in the sun. You must have had terrible dreams. You were always talking about a silver ball and your life's thread.'

'Am I then not old and ill?' asked Peter.

'No,' laughed his mother, 'at the most ill, but that also has passed.'

Peter jumped out of bed and flung his arms round his mother's neck. He looked in his mirror and a pale boyish face laughed back at him.

'And Lisa is not an old woman?' he asked happily.

'Your mind is wandering again,' said his mother fearfully. 'Lisa is sitting outside in the living room, waiting until she can see you. Lisa,' she called.

Lisa came in, secretly wiping away a tear, and gave Peter her hand.

'Oh, Lisa,' cried Peter, 'I am quite well again. Tomorrow morning we will go to school together. And one day you and I will be married. I can hardly wait.'

And as he grasped her hand, Peter noticed with a start of surprise that clinging to his trousers was a tiny piece of golden thread.

The
Three
Oranges

There was once a widow who had three sons. Their father had died when the youngest was still a baby, so she had reared them single-handed. Now they were grown up, and she would have liked them to marry, for she had always wanted daughters, but none of the girls in the village pleased them.

At the edge of the village lived an old woman of whom it was said that ther was more to her than met the eye. On day the three brothers went to her fo help. She was sitting on the doorstep c her little cottage, nursing her cat, and o her shoulder sat an old black crow wit one eye closed. She nodded and smile when she saw the three brothers, an said that she had been expecting them.

She invited them into her cottage, an when they had eaten her rich dark frui cake, and drunk a glass each of her home made nettle beer, she asked what sh could do for them.

'Can't you help us each to find wife?' asked the eldest brother.

'What sort of a wife?' the old woma asked.

The eldest replied, 'For me, a beautifu one.'

'For me, a rich one,' said the second

She asked the youngest one more tha once. He was supposed to be rathe stupid and did not know what to say. A last he said, 'I would like a wife I can lov a great deal, and who will love me i return.'

Then both his brothers started to laugh but the woman said, 'Each one of you will get a wife exactly as you have asked You must, however, stay together an do exactly as I say.'

This they promised, and she continued 'If you travel for three days towards th East, you will reach the castle which ha orange groves. Among all the trees ther is only one which has just three oranges; but these are the biggest and best fruits in the whole garden. You must pick them quickly and quietly, otherwise the owner of this palace will imprison you and you will not be allowed to return home again. You must pick all three at the same time and make sure that you do not hurt the tree. Then bring them to me, and for each orange, I shall present each of you with a wife.'

The three brothers promised to do all this, and then they returned home to their mother and told her all that the old woman had said. She was very pleased, for she herself had found her own husband with the help of the old woman, and had loved him dearly till the day he died. So she said,

'The old woman's advice is sound, my sons. Do exactly as she told you, and each of you will find the wife that you are looking for.'

The brothers were very pleased and excited, and could hardly sleep that night for thinking of their brides. Their mother, too, was delighted, and spent the whole night lying awake and planning the most splendid triple wedding for her sons.

The next day, after a good breakfast, the three young men kissed their mother good-bye and set off on their way to the castle, singing and laughing and leaping over hedges and ditches, and full of joy that at last they should be married.

'My bride will be so beautiful I shall be the envy of the world,' said the eldest brother.

'My bride will be so rich, I shall have everything I desire for the rest of my days, and no one will be wealthier than I,' declared the second brother.

The youngest brother listened to what they had to say, and kept silent. But he

thought, 'My bride will love me, and
her, and no one could make me happie
than I shall be.'

They travelled quite a long way tha
first day and began to think they migh
complete the journey in two days instea
of the three that the old woman had sai
it would take.

They passed through strange countr
side, where the people were small an
swarthy, and wore gold rings in their ear
But they were a peaceable people, an
gave the brothers milk and bread to hel
them on their way. The brothers als
saw many beautiful girls with narro
waists and small, arched feet, but the
gave them not a second glance, for thei
thoughts were only of the three girl
they had been promised.

Then they came to a land where th

people were tall and strong, with flowing golden hair and green-grey stones set in their nostrils. These were a war-like tribe, and hostile to any stranger. The brothers hurried through the towns and villages, keeping to the outskirts and hiding behind hedges when anyone passed. The girls here, too, were beautiful, tall and slim, with soft white shoulders, but their eyes were cold and cruel.

At last night fell, and the three brothers took refuge in a deserted barn, among the field-mice and hedgehogs. They made a fire from twigs and in the doorway of the barn cooked a supper of fish which they had caught in a nearby stream. Then they sat in the firelight watching the midges dancing and the stars weaving patterns in the sky, till the moon was full above them.

It was strange and not a little frightening, to sleep out all night with so much unknown land around them, but they found comfort in one another's presence, and reminded themselves that they would soon be wed.

None of them wanted to sleep that night, for they were quite fearful, alone here in the dark, but at last they built up the fire and settled down to rest in the straw, for they had travelled far and were, indeed, tired.

It took them a long while to drop off to sleep, but eventually, after drinking a bottle of wine each, and singing a few songs, and telling each other how they would have the best wives anyone could find this side of the moon, they fell into a restless doze, to dream of weddings and oranges and strange old women.

Towards the middle of the night a shaft of moonlight shone down through the door of the barn and on to the face of the eldest brother, and at last it woke him up. He saw his brothers sleeping peacefully and thought, 'Why on earth do I need the other two with me? Who knows, we would probably quarrel if we all three arrived back at the old woman's cottage at the same time and were each offered a wife. I shall go and pick an orange for myself. The other two can follow me.' For he had quite forgotten the old woman's warning that all three must stay together.

So he crept quietly away and hurried

so quickly that the next night he had already reached the wonderful castle. The garden lay bathed in the golden evening light. The gate stood open and he crept inside.

No one stirred in the castle. The guard dogs were asleep on their chains and did not so much as stir as he tip-toed past their kennels.

He searched for a long time in the big garden. Then, at last, in the farthest corner, he saw a magnificent tree. It was covered with blossom. Only on a single branch were three big oranges which were ripe. But he could not reach them, and he thought, 'If only my brothers were here, we could climb on one another's shoulders and reach the fruit.'

He tried to climb up, and while doing this he trod with his great heavy boots on some of the lower branches, and as he stretched out his hand towards the first orange he suddenly found he could not move. The tree held him fast and he could not climb down.

He wanted to cry out, but was afraid of waking the guard dogs and the sleeping inhabitants of the castle. So he stayed quite still for a long time and was growing very stiff and uncomfortable when, suddenly, the castle came alive.

Servants came hurrying, followed by an old man who touched him with a stick. Then the tree let go of him and he was able to climb down again. The guard dogs broke their chains and came yapping

and snapping round his ankles. The old
man waved his stick in the air, while the
servants shouted, and cursed the brother
for a trespasser and a thief.

Then the servants caught hold of him
and took him to a cellar in the depths of
the castle where he was kept prisoner.

When the two brothers noticed that
their eldest brother had left them, they
continued on their way alone.

During the second night the second
brother was unable to sleep. He looked at
his young brother, who was sleeping
peacefully beside him and thought, 'I
am sure our brother has gone ahead to
the castle. I must hurry so that I may
find him again. Our young brother is
stupid, he would only spoil everything.
I think I shall go on my own.'

He then crept quietly away and hurried
all through the rest of the night and
reached the castle the next morning.
Again all was quiet, the gate was open
and the oranges glittered in the dawn
light. The guard dogs were back on their
chains, and they were still sleeping so
did not hear him pass. He saw traces of
footprints in the grass and they led to
the tree with the three beautiful oranges
hanging on the branch. He saw them
hanging above him, but could not reach
them, and thought, 'If only two of us
were here, one of us could climb on to the
shoulders of the other.'

He noticed the bent branches, but he
did not dare to climb up. However, as he

was looking round, he noticed a long pole lying on the grass. Quickly he grabbed it, and gave the branch with the three oranges a hard blow. But the oranges did not fall down, and instead he heard voices coming from the tree which moaned and groaned.

Suddenly the castle came alive. Servants came hurrying, took him prisoner, and put him down into the cellar to join his brother.

When the youngest brother awoke, he found the second brother also gone. He shook his head sadly and thought, 'I must hurry to find the castle. Perhaps my brothers have been taken prisoner. I must help them.'

He travelled all day, and in the evening he arrived at the castle. The gate was open; silence reigned everywhere. The dogs were nowhere to be seen. He found footprints of his brothers among the blossom in the long, damp grass, and he saw the branch which carried the three magnificent oranges. He looked up and thought, 'Whatever happens, I must not harm the tree.'

The three oranges seemed to mesmerise him, and as he looked at them he realised he must hurry. He took a running jump, caught hold of the branch and pulled it down towards him. It broke. The tree started to moan. The castle door opened, and an old man came out slowly, looking sad and serious.

'Now you have the branch with its

three oranges,' he said, 'I can do no harm to you, but because you tore the branch down you will suffer a great deal.' Then he turned round, went back into the castle, and disappeared through the door.

The youngest brother went carefully into the castle and soon he noticed that every door opened of its own accord when he touched it with the branch.

At length he reached the cellar and found his brothers. They were very ashamed and did not say much, but he was so pleased to see them again that he was not angry with them. There were three loaves and three bottles of red wine on a board in the cellar, and as they had finished their provisions, each one of them

took a loaf and a bottle of wine and then they started on their homeward journey.

On the way the eldest brothers became hungry and thirsty. So they ate their bread and drank the wine. The youngest refreshed himself by merely smelling the lovely scent of the oranges which he was carefully carrying. Then he noticed that the branch on which they were still hanging had not withered at all in spite of the heat, but still looked fresh and new.

During the night, the eldest brother could not sleep. Quietly he went over to the branch and took off one of the oranges. Then he crept out and started on the way home by himself. As he was

hurrying along to reach the old woman, the sun was so hot that he became very thirsty. It seemed as if he had completely lost his way and would die of thirst. He took his orange and cut it in half. And there before him stood a most beautiful young girl who asked, 'Have you any bread?'

'No,' he said, 'I have eaten it.'

'Have you any wine?' she asked.

'No,' he said, 'I have drunk it.'

So she said, 'In that case I shall go back into my orange and back on to the tree.' And as she said this she disappeared, and so did the orange.

Then the eldest brother was suddenly filled with a tremendous desire to find her again, and he hurried back the way he had come. He did not meet his brothers, and he wandered about some-

what at a loss. Eventually he found the way back to the castle, only to be immediately captured by the servants and locked in the cellar.

The same thing happened to the second brother. He could not wait, stole the second orange off the branch which his brother was holding in his hand as he lay sleeping, and hurried away with it towards home. He became very thirsty, could not find a spring, and at last he halved his orange. At once a young girl stood before him. She was very richly dressed and had a pearl necklace round her throat, rings on her fingers, expensive ear-rings and golden bracelets.

'Have you any bread?' she asked.

'No,' he answered, 'I have eaten it.'

'Have you any wine?' she said.

'No,' he answered, 'I have drunk it.'

So she said, 'In that case I shall go back into my orange and back onto the tree.' And as she said this she disappeared together with the orange.

Then the second brother was filled with a tremendous desire to find this girl again and he hurried back the way he had come. He did not meet the youngest brother. He wandered about, not knowing which way to go, and when he finally found his way back to the castle, he was taken prisoner by the servants and locked into the cellar with his brother.

When the youngest brother awoke and saw that his brothers had disappeared and that only one orange remained on the branch, he thought, 'Now my brothers have gone on ahead to the old woman. I must hurry and follow them.'

As he was going along he became hungry and thirsty, but he decided to be satisfied with the smell of the orange. This made him feel quite drunk, and he had a tremendous urge to eat the fruit. He took it and cut it open. At once a young girl stood before him, simply dressed with hair hanging over her shoulders. She looked at him in such a friendly way that he immediately fell in love with her.

'Have you any bread?' she asked.

'Yes,' he said, and gave it to her.

'Have you any wine?' she asked.

'Yes,' he said, and opened the bottle, poured the red wine and offered it to her.

'Now we shall be happy,' she said, offering him the wine, and they both drank.

When she had eaten a little of the bread he said, 'Now we shall both go to my home.'

'Don't forget the branch,' she said, 'for without it I must return to the tree,' and he took it and they started on their way.

As they passed the house of the old woman, she was standing at her door and looking towards the youngest brother.

'Where are the others?' she asked.

He told her all that had happened. Then she said, 'You tore off the branch, and because of this you will have much unhappiness. But you have found for yourself a charming bride.' And she went to embrace and kiss the girl. And as she did this she secretly took an embroidery needle from her pocket and stuck it in the back of the girl's neck. The youngest brother did not see it but suddenly the girl gave a cry, and in the same moment she turned into a white dove and started fluttering round the young man.

The old woman had disappeared. In vain the young man looked for her and

the girl. At last he went to his mother to tell her everything, and ask for her advice. And because the dove did not cease to flutter round him, he took it on his shoulder and brought it home. His mother was pleased that at least one of her sons had returned to her, but she was very sad about the other two, and they often spoke about them and wondered if they would ever be found.

The youngest brother mourned bitterly for his lovely bride, and wondered where she could be. He had been promised much unhappiness, and this he was surely suffering, but had not the old woman also promised that he should have the bride of his desiring? Where, then, was she? Both he and his mother loved the little dove very much. It never flew away, but was always with them, and at every meal it took small bits and pieces of food from them.

The mother noticed that the dove was often scratching the back of its head with one foot. She wondered what there could be wrong with it. One day the dove perched on her knee, and she noticed the needle. Then she called her son and

said: 'Look, a needle! Who on earth would have been so cruel as to do that?' and she pulled the needle out very carefully. Hardly had she done so than the dove changed back into the girl, and the youngest son called out: 'This is my bride!'

Then all three were very happy, but the girl said, 'Where is the branch?'

'I have thrown it away,' said the mother, 'on to the rubbish heap.'

They hurried behind the house and searched through all the rubbish, but they could not find the branch.

'In that case,' said the girl, 'I must return home, for my sisters will still be trapped inside the oranges.'

The mother gave them directions and in less than two days they were at the gate of the garden. And there, on the big tree, was the branch. It had grown on to the tree again, and on it were the two oranges. The big stick was also nearby, but the young man did not take it. Instead he knelt down at the foot of the tree and said to the girl, 'Stand on my shoulders.'

This she did, and when he stood up she stretched upwards and carefully picked the two oranges, and hardly had she jumped down with them than the two oranges changed into the two other girls.

Then the door of the castle opened. The old man came out with his servants and they had with them the two brothers.

The bride of the youngest one put her hands into those of her two sisters.

But the owner of the castle went towards the tree, touched the branch with his stick, and it immediately broke away. The old man caught it and it was straightway changed into a beautiful lady. She was the girls' mother, and the wife of the castle-owner. He had once in anger cast a spell on them and changed the woman and her daughters into the branch and the oranges. But now they were free. Th mother of the three brothers was sen for and they then celebrated the tripl wedding.

Now the three brothers were happ for as each one had made his wish so h obtained the bride he had wanted. Bu the happiest of the brothers was th youngest. For beauty fades, riches alway bring worries and only true love stay the same for ever.